The New Adventures of

MARY-KATE & ASHLEY™

The Case Of The

Logical I Ranch

Look for more great books in

series:

The Case Of The Great Elephant Escape
The Case Of The Summer Camp Caper
The Case Of The Surfing Secret
The Case Of The Green Ghost
The Case Of The Big Scare Mountain Mystery
The Case Of The Slam Dunk Mystery
The Case Of The Rock Star's Secret
The Case Of The Cheerleading Camp Mystery
The Case Of The Flying Phantom
The Case Of The Creepy Castle
The Case Of The Golden Slipper
The Case Of The Flapper 'Napper
The Case Of The High Seas Secret

and coming soon

The Case Of The Dog Camp Mystery

The Case Of The Logical I Ranch

by Pauline Preiss

HarperEntertainment
An Imprint of HarperCollins*Publishers*

A PARACHUTE PRESS BOOK

Parachute Publishing, L.L.C.
156 Fifth Avenue
New York, NY 10010

Dualstar Publications
c/o Thorne and Company
A Professional Law Corporation
1801 Century Park East
Los Angeles, CA 90067

HarperEntertainment

An Imprint of HarperCollins*Publishers*
10 East 53rd Street, New York, NY 10022

For information, address HarperCollins Publishers Inc.
10 East 53rd Street, New York, NY 10022

ISBN 0-06-106645-1

First printing: May 2001

Printed in the United States of America

10 9 8 7 6 5 4 3 2 1

1

HOME ON THE RANGE

"I'm bored," said my twin sister, Ashley.

"Want to play some board games?" I asked. "Get it? *Board* games?"

Ashley rolled her eyes. "Ha, ha, Mary-Kate. We've already played every board game in the house. Plus six games of checkers. And I don't even *like* checkers!"

It was summer vacation. A beautiful, sunny afternoon. Great, huh?

Sure, great—*if* you're at the beach, like our friend Samantha Samuels.

Or *if* you're traveling to the Grand Canyon, like our pal Tim Park.

But we weren't going anywhere cool anytime soon. We were stuck at home while almost all our friends were away. And there wasn't a whole lot to do.

Ashley and I are detectives. We run the Olsen and Olsen Mystery Agency out of our attic. We love to solve mysteries.

But we can't solve one if we don't have one!

Business was slow. In fact, it was so slow, it had stopped.

We'd played games. Watched TV. Gone bike riding. We'd even—eww!—cleaned up our room! Now, *that's* bored!

I flopped back on a bean bag chair and stared at the clock on the wall. "I'm going to investigate how long it takes the second hand to go around one full time."

Then the phone rang.

"I've got it!" Ashley and I shouted at the

same time. I picked up the blue phone. Ashley grabbed the pink one.

"Hello? Hello?" we heard someone say.

"Olsen and Olsen Mystery Agency!" we both answered.

"If you've got a crime," I added, "we've *definitely* got the time!"

"Hi, guys. It's me, Patty."

Ashley covered her phone with her hand. We both sighed.

Patty O'Leary lives next door to us. We call her "Princess Patty" because she acts like a princess. She's used to getting her own way all the time.

"Guess what?" Patty exclaimed. "My uncle Josh just quit his job."

"Oh, that's too bad," Ashley said.

"No, it's good," Patty said. "He and his two pals just bought a dude ranch."

"Dude ranch?" I repeated.

"You know, a place where people pay to do cowboy things," Ashley said. "Like riding horses. Rounding up cows. Singing cowboy songs around a campfire..."

"Isn't that cool?" Patty asked.

"That's nice," Ashley said politely.

"And guess what?" Patty went on. "My uncle invited me to come to the grand opening."

"Terrific," I said grumpily. Even Princess Patty got to go someplace cool!

"And I get to bring two friends," Patty added.

"Reeeally?" I said hopefully.

Ashley and I crossed our fingers.

"All my other friends are away on vacation," Patty said. "So I thought maybe you two could come."

It was a rude way to invite us. But that's Patty for you. And I really wanted to go! I started to shout "You bet!" but Ashley waved at me to be quiet.

"We need to check our calendar," Ashley said. Her voice was businesslike. I tried not to giggle as she flipped through our date book. All the days were totally blank.

"We just happen to be in between cases at the moment," Ashley told Patty.

I smothered a laugh with both hands.

"So, do you guys want to go?" Patty asked.

"Yeah!" I exclaimed.

"We'd love to," Ashley said. "Thank you."

"Great," Patty replied. "I'll have my mom and dad call your mom and dad. Oh, and one more thing. I just got new cowboy boots. They're red. So if you get boots—get another color."

I rolled my eyes. Same old Patty.

We hung up. Ashley and I gave each other a high five. "Yee-haw!" we shouted.

Patty's parents talked to our parents and worked everything out. We left for the ranch the very next morning.

Patty's uncle picked us up at the airport.

He was dressed head to toe in cowboy gear: ten-gallon hat, red checked shirt, and big black cowboy boots.

"Howdy, partners!" Uncle Josh hollered. Then he added, "That's cowboy talk for hello."

Ashley and I giggled.

"We know," Patty said.

Uncle Josh put our bags in his truck. Then we drove off. I rolled down my window and took a deep breath of desert air.

"Put the air-conditioning on, Uncle Josh," Patty whined. "It's so hot! And my hair's getting messed up by the wind!"

I sighed and rolled my window back up.

"Wait till you see the Logical I Ranch!" Uncle Josh said. "It's the prettiest little ranch in the whole wide West."

"Logical I? That's a weird name for a ranch," Patty said.

"Yeah. How did you come up with it?" Ashley asked.

"Well, we found this old map of the place," Josh explained. "It was torn and faded. But that's what it said at the top: Logical I. Kind of like the Lazy B, or the Crooked R."

"Cool," I said. It sounded so mysterious!

"We figured that was the name of the ranch a long time ago," Uncle Josh said. "So we decided to use it. We were going to hang the map up in the main lobby," he added. "But, well, somehow we must have misplaced it."

"A mystery?" I whispered to Ashley.

She shook her head. "I doubt it."

I looked out the truck window. The landscape was just like in an old western movie—lots of cactuses, big tumbleweeds rolling across the road, and miles and miles of sky.

"I grew up watching cowboys in the movies, and cowboys on TV," Uncle Josh told us. "I always wanted to be one when I

grew up." He laughed. "I finally got my wish. It's a dream come true."

At last we arrived at the ranch. It looked as if it came straight out of an old western movie. It was at the end of a long, dusty road. In front of the main house, or lodge, was an old-fashioned well. The guest rooms were in several buildings off to the right of the lodge, with signs that said BUNKHOUSE. Out in back I could see a barn with a fenced-in yard.

"That's the corral," Uncle Josh said. "I'll give you a tour so you can see it all."

"Look!" Ashley said as we pulled up in front of the lodge. "The guests are all dressed up like cowboys!"

I noticed they all were carrying suitcases. "Wow!" I exclaimed. "They must all be checking in!"

"I hope they didn't give away my room," Patty said. She looked worried.

But then Ashley poked me in the ribs.

“Look, Mary-Kate,” she whispered.

I looked more closely. None of the guests were smiling. In fact, they all looked angry! I watched a man and woman dragging their suitcases toward the parking lot. Both of them were scowling.

I glanced at Uncle Josh. He had a worried look on his face.

Just then the front door flew open. A man with two suitcases stomped out. A woman and three boys followed him.

“We’re leaving!” the man shouted. I could hear him even though the truck windows were closed.

“They’re not checking in,” Ashley said. “They’re checking *out*!”

“What’s going on?” Princess Patty asked.

“I don’t know,” I said. “But something is very wrong!”

2

A Ten-Gallon Problem

We jumped out of the truck.

Ewwwww! What was that awful smell?

Ashley and I held our noses. We didn't want to say anything that might sound rude. But Patty wasn't so tongue-tied.

"Gross!" she shrieked. "This place stinks!" She waved her hand in front of her face. "It smells like rotten eggs!"

We watched a man and woman screech off in their car. Uncle Josh stood there in a cloud of dust. He looked totally confused.

Two men hurried out to meet him. One was big and dark-haired. The other one was short and slim with curly brown hair.

"What's up, George?" Uncle Josh asked the big man.

George shook his head. "Same thing, Josh," he said sadly. "The well!"

Patty waved the air in front of her face. "That smell is coming from the well? It smells like a dead skunk!"

The other man, Slim, nodded his head. "Every now and then, that awful smell comes out of our well." He held his nose.

"So the stuff we put down there didn't help at all, huh?" Uncle Josh said.

"Nope," George replied. "The smell is even worse."

"But that's not all," Slim said. "There's a lot more strange things going on."

"Like what?" Uncle Josh asked. He looked even more worried.

"At breakfast, several guests complained

of rumbling under the bunkhouses," Slim continued.

"And somebody reported heavy black smoke floating past their bunk," George added. "We checked it out, but we couldn't find anything burning."

"Now some of the guests are leaving!" Slim said. "They want their money back!"

"I don't blame them," Patty said. "Pee-yew!"

Uncle Josh shook his head. "I can't believe the bad luck we've been having ever since we opened the place. Why, it's almost as if somebody's trying to drive us away!"

Ashley poked me in the ribs. "Did you hear that?"

I nodded. I knew we were both thinking the same thing.

"Hear what?" Patty asked. She covered her nose and mouth with her purple bandanna and smoothed her hair.

"It sounds like a mystery!" I exclaimed.

Patty made a face. "Oh, please. It's just an old well with smelly water."

I turned to Uncle Josh. "Do you really think someone wants you to leave the ranch?" I asked. "Maybe we can help."

Uncle Josh smiled. "Patty told me you two were detectives."

Ashley carries her detective notebook and a pencil with her wherever she goes. She pulled them out of her back pocket and got ready to write.

"Who do you think might be trying to harm the ranch?" Ashley asked. "And why?"

Uncle Josh shook his head. "I appreciate the offer of help. But I didn't really mean what I said. I don't think there's any mystery here. Just a lot of bad luck." Before I could start to argue, he turned to Slim. "Slim, you come with me. Let's see if we can't close off the well somehow. Maybe that will help. George, you see if you can

calm down the guests. Tell them the problem will be fixed very soon. And remind them about the big barn dance tonight."

He looked at us apologetically. "Sorry, kids. That tour will have to wait. We've got an emergency."

"Don't worry," I said. "Let us know if we can help."

"Thanks," Uncle Josh said. "I wish you could. But I'm afraid there's nothing you can do."

Then he and his buddies hurried off.

I shook my head in disappointment. "I thought we had a case here for sure."

"Me, too," Ashley said. "Let's keep our eyes and ears open."

"Come on, you guys," Patty said. "I'm tired. And hungry. *And* I want to see my room."

Ashley and I grabbed our bags and followed Patty to our bunkhouse. It had bunk beds and chests of drawers for our things.

On the wall hung a picture of a cowboy kissing his horse.

"Neat!" Ashley said as we went inside.

"Cool!" I said. "Can I have the top bunk?"

"Ugh!" Patty complained. "There's no air-conditioning!"

Ashley and I both sighed. Sharing a bunk with Patty was not going to be easy!

Uncle Josh and his partners sealed off the well with a big rock. The breeze blew the bad smell away. Patty cheered up. And most of the guests decided to stay.

I was still disappointed we didn't have a case. But I was ready to have some fun! "Let's go ride horses!" I said.

We ran to the horse barn, which was behind the main lodge. Nearby, several kids were riding horses around the corral. Other kids sat on the fence, waiting for a turn.

"I ride English style, not Western," Patty sniffed.

"Come on, Patty," Ashley said. "This is a ranch. It'll be fun!"

"I guess," Patty grumbled.

We sat on the fence and waited our turn. I loved this place already. The weather was warm and sunny. The horses were beautiful. I could live here all summer! Even Patty was starting to look excited. "I'm dying to ride that white horse!" she said.

Something beeped next to us. We all looked over. A redheaded boy sitting on the railing beside Patty was playing an electronic game.

He wasn't wearing any cowboy gear. Instead he had on shorts and tennis shoes.

Patty's eyes lit up. She tossed her brown hair. "Excuse me," she said, fluttering her eyelashes at him. "I think you're next."

He didn't take his eyes off the game. "You go ahead. I'm not really interested in riding horses."

"Me, either," Patty said quickly.

Not interested? Two minutes ago she was dying to ride!

Patty scooted over closer to the boy. "I'm Patty," she said. "What's your name?"

This time the boy did glance up from his game. He looked kind of annoyed. "Andrew," he said.

"My uncle owns this ranch," Patty boasted. "He let me bring my friends here on vacation for free." She waved a hand at Ashley and me.

"Your uncle owns this dump?" Andrew said, sneering at Patty.

"Dump?" I said. That made me mad. "The Logical I is so cool!"

"Huh!" Andrew snorted. "Ranches are for losers. If I owned this place I'd sell all the horses and make it into a huge virtual reality game space." He slid down from the fence.

Patty looked kind of embarrassed for a minute. But then she nodded. "Totally!" she

agreed. "I hate ranches, too. You know, I told Uncle Josh he should do something else with this place."

I shook my head. I couldn't believe what I was hearing!

Patty slid down, too. "A game space is a great idea! Um—what kind of games did you say, again?" she asked.

Andrew rolled his eyes. "Virtual reality! Don't you know anything about computer games?" He started to walk away.

Patty followed him. I heard her say, "I love computer games! I'm really good at Pac-man."

"Pac-man!" Andrew said. "No, no, I'm talking about serious stuff. Online games that you play with a bunch of people...."

His voice faded as they got farther away. Ashley and I looked at each other.

"I think Patty likes him." I laughed.

"Come on," Ashley said with a grin. "Let's ride!"

* * *

After our rides, Ashley and I decided to go to the lodge and get something to drink. But as we neared the back of the lodge, we heard loud voices coming from Uncle Josh's office!

I hurried over and stood under the open window.

Ashley raced up behind me. "We really shouldn't eavesdrop on the conversation," she whispered. "It's not polite."

I bent down on one knee. "I'm not," I said. "I'm just stopping to tie my shoe."

Ashley stared at me. "You're wearing cowboy boots!"

"Shhh!" I told her.

The shouting grew louder. A man was inside, yelling at Uncle Josh.

"A cowboy theme park would be perfect here," he argued. "It would bring lots of tourists. It will create new jobs."

"What part of 'no' don't you understand,

Mr. Cunningham?" Uncle Josh said.

"I'm offering you an awful lot of money for this lonely patch of dry, dusty desert," Mr. Cunningham growled. "You'd be a *fool* not to sell!"

"I've told you, Mr. Cunningham. The Logical I Ranch is not for sale."

I heard more arguing. Then I heard Mr. Cunningham shout, "I'll get this ranch—one way or another!"

Then we heard a door slam.

Ashley and I rushed around the corner of the lodge. We caught sight of a short bald man in a suit. He was stomping away from the building.

Ashley pulled out her notebook. "I know Patty's uncle doesn't think there's any mystery here, but maybe he's wrong. I think we've got a case, Mary-Kate!"

I nodded. "And Mr. Cunningham is our number-one suspect!"

3

Stirring Up Trouble

"Right!" Ashley said. She began to write in her notebook. "Mr. Cunningham wants to buy the ranch, bad. He said he'd pay any price. But Uncle Josh won't sell. Maybe Mr. Cunningham is trying to scare people away so the ranch will go out of business. Then he can buy it to build a theme park here."

I nodded. "Let's follow him and see if we can find out more!" I said.

We ran after Mr. Cunningham. But then

we saw him get in a silver truck. He gunned the motor, backed up, and drove away.

Ashley and I looked at each other and groaned.

"He's probably heading back to town," I said. "We've got a case and a suspect…"

"But how can we investigate him," Ashley said, "if he's gone?"

That night we got dressed up in denim skirts, cowboy hats, and boots. Then we headed to the barn dance. "Come on, cowboys and cowgirls!" Uncle Josh's voice boomed from the loudspeakers. "Come to the hoedown!"

The dance was held in a great big barn decorated with lots of red-and-white streamers. There were hay bales to sit on and a long wooden table with picnic food on it. At the far end, a fiddler was playing some cheerful music, and lots of people were dancing.

Patty was showing off steps from her dance recital. I had to laugh. I'd never seen a tap-dancing cowgirl before.

A few minutes later, she came up to us. "Having fun?" I asked her.

"I guess," she said. She was staring across the room. I followed her gaze.

Andrew was leaning against a wall, playing his handheld video game again.

"He needs someone to dance with," Patty said. She marched up to him. Ashley and I followed.

"Hi, Andrew," she said.

He barely even looked up. "Shhhh! I'm right in the middle of a serious game of Ninja Warriors. It's so cool! I'm online with three of my friends right now!"

"Want to dance?" Patty asked.

I have to admit I was impressed. I'm not sure I'd be able to ask a boy to dance just like that!

Andrew's face turned red. "Um—I

don't—" he began.

"Don't worry, I'll teach you," Patty interrupted. "I'm a really good dancer, you know."

Andrew frowned. "But I—"

"Come on," Patty said, grabbing his arm. "They're starting a new song!"

Ashley and I watched as Patty pulled Andrew out onto the dance floor. We could see her pointing to his feet and telling him where to put them.

"Oh, boy. Now he looks *totally* miserable!" Ashley said as we walked over to the refreshment table.

"Yeah. He doesn't like this place to start with," I said. "And now he's stuck dancing with Patty, too!"

"Better him than us," Ashley said with a grin.

"Hey, Ashley," I said, as an idea struck me. "You don't think Andrew could be behind the weird stuff here, do you? I mean, he really doesn't like the Logical I."

Ashley shook her head. "That's true, but Uncle Josh said the weird things have been happening ever since they opened the place, remember? And Andrew has only been here for a couple of days."

"I guess you're right," I said.

A few minutes later, Uncle Josh, George, and Slim went up on the stage. Slim played the fiddle while they sang cowboy songs like "Home on the Range." We all sang along. And then we danced some more. It was so much fun!

Before we knew it, it was ten o'clock. Ashley took off her hat and fanned herself. "Excuse me," she said, yawning. "I'm plumb tuckered out."

I looked around. The band was shutting down for the night. People were getting ready to go. Uncle Josh was sitting in a nearby chair, yawning.

All of a sudden the big wooden door flew open. An old man with a long gray beard stomped in. His clothes were dirty and his face was smudged. The only things on him that looked clean were his shiny black rubber boots. In his hand was a large rolled-up sheet of paper. I could see that the paper was yellow and the ink was faded.

"You all better watch out!" the old man shouted. "You better watch out for the dragon!"

Huh? Dragon? My ears perked up.

"Oh, no! Not this again," I heard Uncle Josh mutter. Then he jumped up from his chair and ran over to meet the man at the door. "Howdy, Dusty!" he called loudly. He turned to the guests. "Everybody, I'd like you to meet Dusty Jones. He's been around these parts for years and years. He used to help out here when it was a real working ranch."

Dusty nodded. "Been here longer than I can remember," he said. "That's why you folks can believe me when I tell you this." His eyes grew wide. "All the funny smells and smoke and stuff around here? That's all caused by a dragon. So keep your eyes peeled!"

Uncle Josh looked a little annoyed, but he laughed. "Okay, Dusty, we'll be careful." He turned to the crowd and winked. "Right, folks?"

Lots of people laughed. I think they thought Dusty was just part of the barn dance show.

"You bet!" a man in a yellow cowboy hat said.

"Don't worry," a woman behind him said. "I've got some dragon repellent in my purse."

"She's making that up," I said to Ashley. "There's no such thing as dragon repellent."

"Mary-Kate, there's no such thing as dragons!" Ashley reminded me.

"I know that," I muttered.

Then Andrew, who was standing nearby, spoke up. "He could be right, you know," he said. "I read on the Internet about how some people in Russia found a dragon. They showed pictures of it online! It had wings, and it was breathing fire!"

"Really?" I said. I wanted to see those pictures.

"Now, Andrew," his father said. "That was a joke. You know there's no such thing as dragons."

Andrew shook his head. "I'm not so sure!"

"Me, either!" Patty announced.

"Smart kids," Dusty said. "Maybe the dragon won't get *them*!"

Uncle Josh winced. He looked as if he was getting a headache. "Come on over to the refreshment table, Dusty," he said. "The fried chicken is mighty tasty."

Dusty sniffed. "Don't mind if I do."

Ashley stared after Dusty as he walked

away. She had one line across her forehead. I know that line. She gets it when she's thinking hard.

"I think we should talk to Dusty," she said.

"How come?" I asked. "You don't believe his dragon story, do you?"

Ashley shook her head. "No way. But Dusty's been around the ranch a long time. Maybe he knows something that will help us crack this case."

"Makes sense," I said. "Let's go."

I walked up to Dusty and stuck out my hand. "Hi. My name is Mary-Kate Olsen," I said. "And this is my sister, Ashley."

Dusty put down his chicken leg, wiped his hand off on his pants, and gave mine a shake. "My real name's Abraham Lincoln Jones," he said. "Dusty's my nickname."

"Dusty," Ashley said. "How did you get that nickname?"

I wouldn't have thought to ask a question like that. It seemed pretty obvious to me. He was covered with dust. Even his glasses were dusty.

"Used to work in the oil fields," Dusty said. "You get pretty dusty out there."

"Used to?" I said. I couldn't help noticing he still had a lot of dust on his clothes. "How long has it been since you worked in the oil fields?"

"About twenty years," Dusty said.

My eyes popped open. Ashley's eyebrows shot up.

Dusty chuckled. "Being dusty is kind of a habit with me," he said with a shrug. "After I quit the oil business, I worked on the Logical I Ranch for old Mr. McKee. When he sold the place, the new owners let me stay on."

"What do you do now?" Ashley asked.

"I follow the creeks, panning for gold with this here map!" He waved the rolled-up piece of paper at us.

So that's why he was wearing rubber

boots. I could imagine him following the little blue lines on the map in search of tiny nuggets of gold. The Logical I was a big ranch. It would take a person years to explore every inch of it.

"Did you actually find gold?" I asked excitedly.

"No," he told me. He tossed the chicken bone over his shoulder. Then he stared at me through narrowed eyes. "I found a dragon instead!"

Ashley frowned. "There's no such thing as dragons."

That seemed to make Dusty really mad. "Oh, no?" he snapped. He waved the rolled-up map under Ashley's nose. "Let me tell you something, young lady. There's a real dragon wandering this ranch. And I can prove it!"

4

Following the Footprints

I reached out to take the map from Dusty. Did that old piece of paper prove there was a real live dragon? Then I wanted to see it!

But Dusty jerked the map away from me and leaped up from his chair. "Not on your life!" he snapped. "This here is my map, and I ain't sharing!"

He hurried out the door.

Ashley stared after him. "That was really weird," she said.

"Do you think Dusty is a suspect?" I

asked. "Could he be trying to scare people off the ranch with this dragon story?"

"I don't know," Ashley said. "What could his motive be?"

Motive means a person's reason for doing something. It's a word our great-grandma Olive taught us. She's a detective, too.

I shook my head. "I don't know. But we should check him out."

"Right," Ashley agreed. "Let's talk to him in the morning."

We started to walk back to our bunkhouse. It was pretty dark.

I pulled out my little flashlight and shone it down at the ground so we could see where we were going.

"Hey, look!" I said. There were lots of footprints in the dust. Mostly they were pointy-toed cowboy boot prints.

But one set of footprints was different. They were round-toed. The soles had a wavy pattern on them.

"Those prints are from Dusty's rubber boots!" I exclaimed, pointing at them. "Ashley, look where they're going! Straight toward the smelly well!"

"Come on!" she said, grabbing my arm. "Let's go see what he's up to!"

We hurried toward the old well, following Dusty's tracks. But about ten feet in front of it, the footprints turned to the left.

Ashley stopped and stared. "Where could he be going? I don't think there's anything over that way except cactuses."

"Let's keep following the footprints and find out," I suggested.

We kept walking. The footprints led us down into a dry streambed. Soon we couldn't see the lights from the lodge.

My flashlight made a bouncing circle of light on the ground. Other than that, it was totally dark. And totally quiet.

"Th-this is kind of creepy," I whispered.

"What if we get lost out here?"

"Don't worry," Ashley said. "We can always follow Dusty's footprints back to the lodge, remember?"

That made me feel better. I'm glad Ashley is so logical.

I peered down at the ground. Now I wanted to make double sure we didn't lose Dusty's trail.

Then I froze.

One step later, Ashley stopped, too.

"What in the world is *that*?" she gasped.

There in the hard, dusty ground was one of Dusty's boot prints. And next to it was the biggest footprint I had ever seen!

It wasn't a person's footprint.

Not with claws like that.

"Oh, my gosh!" I exclaimed. Maybe Dusty wasn't making things up after all.

Because that huge track sure looked like a dragon footprint to me!

5

A NARROW ESCAPE

Ashley got down on her knees. She studied the big footprint without saying a word.

"Well?" I whispered. "What do you think? Is it from a dragon?"

Ashley slowly shook her head. "It sure looks like it. But it *can't* be," she said. Then she pulled out her notebook. "Mary-Kate, hold the flashlight steady."

I held the light on her notebook. She took out her pencil and made a quick sketch of the giant print. I noticed that she sketched in Dusty's boot print next to the dragon print. "That's to show how big the print is," she explained.

It was huge. About three times as big as Dusty's foot!

"We've just got to get a look at Dusty's map!" Ashley said. "If there really is something on the map that proves there's a dragon around here..."

Luckily, Dusty's tracks headed back toward the lodge. A few minutes later we came to an old shack just on the edge of the ranch. A dusty mailbox stood in front. It said A. L. Jones.

"Abraham Lincoln Jones," Ashley said. "Dusty's real name."

Together we crept up to the front door. We knew Dusty had to be inside, because his footprints stopped right at the front porch. And there was a dim light inside.

We sneaked onto the porch and peeked in the window.

The shack had just one room. The light came from an old-fashioned kerosene lamp. It was still lit. But I could see Dusty lying in bed, fast asleep.

I saw the map, too. It was sticking out from under Dusty's pillow.

"How are we going to look at the map?" Ashley whispered. "It's right under his head! Maybe we should wait until morning and then see if he'll show it to us."

I shook my head. "He wouldn't show us the map tonight. Why would he change his mind in the morning?" I argued. "Besides, I can't wait that long. I'll just go in and borrow it for a minute." I turned back to Ashley. "You stay out here and stand guard." I gave the front door a little push.

It wasn't locked. It opened.

Ashley looked nervous. But I just gave her the thumbs-up sign and slipped inside. Then I pushed the door almost closed.

I scuffed along very softly. My boots

barely made a noise. I had to be careful not to trip on anything.

I was almost at Dusty's bed when the toe of my boot hit something. It felt soft, like a pile of laundry. I reached down to shove it out of the way.

Uh-oh! It was big—and furry!

And it started growling!

"Help!" I gasped. I yanked open the front door and dived outside. I crashed right into Ashley, who was coming toward the door.

"Close that door!" I whispered. She reached around me and pulled it shut—just as a huge black dog leaped from inside. It yelped when it hit the door, then barked wildly.

Inside the shack, Dusty began to holler at the dog.

"Run!" I told Ashley.

But we were only halfway across the yard when I heard the door open. I grabbed Ashley's arm and pulled her behind Dusty's old pickup truck. We peeked back at the house.

Dusty was standing in the open doorway. He held his dog by the collar. "Who's there?" he yelled. He held up the kerosene lamp. I could see he was squinting.

"Dusty's not wearing his glasses," I whispered.

"Whew!" Ashley said. "Now he won't be able to see us."

Dusty stood there for another minute or two. I crossed my fingers, hoping he didn't let go of his dog's collar.

Luckily, he didn't. Ashley and I kept as still and silent as we could. After a moment, Dusty stepped back inside. "Dumb dog," we heard him grumble. "Didn't I tell you not to eat them leftover beans? Beans always give you nightmares." Then the door slammed.

I let out a long breath. Then we slipped away, back to our bunkhouse.

"Sorry I didn't get the map," I said when we were safe in our bunks.

"Don't worry about it. We'll talk to Dusty tomorrow," Ashley said. "Let's go to sleep. I'm beat."

"Me, too," I said. "I've had enough adventures for one night."

I fell asleep pretty fast. But a few hours later, a horrible sound woke me up.

My eyes popped open. It was still dark, but the moon was up now. A beam of light lay across the bunkhouse floor.

Then I heard it again. *AAUUGGHH... AAAUUUGGHH!*

It sounded like a huge beast, roaring!

"The dragon!" I gasped.

6

AAUUGGHH!!

I jumped off the top bunk and crawled into bed with Ashley.

"N-now do you believe in dragons?" I asked.

"N-n-no," she stammered back.

"So…what *was* that?" I asked.

"I don't know," she whispered. "But it sure *sounded* like a dragon."

"AAUUGGHH! AAAUUUGGHH!" There it was again!

And then—*"Zzzz-zzzz."*

I clutched Ashley's arm. "What was *that*?"

She pointed at the next bunk. "Patty is snoring," she whispered.

I couldn't believe it. Patty was sleeping right through all this noise!

Ashley threw back the covers. "Come on. We've got to check out that noise."

I gulped. "All right," I whispered.

We climbed out of bed. I was still in my pajamas. Ashley was still in her nightgown. But we didn't have time to change. We just stepped outside.

The deep, eerie roar echoed through the night again. I could see lights going on in the other bunkhouses. A couple of doors opened, and people stuck their heads out.

"AAUUGGHH! AAAUUUGGHH!"

Ashley and I clutched each other's hands and slowly walked toward the sound. I stared around. I didn't see any dragon shapes in the dark night.

"AAUUGGHH! AAAUUUGGHH!"

Now the sound seemed to be behind us!

We turned around—and almost crashed into Uncle Josh. He stood there in his pajamas and cowboy boots. George was right behind him. George clutched a baseball bat in one hand. He looked terrified.

"AAUUGGHH! AAAUUUGGHH!"

"What on earth is that horrible sound?" a woman's voice cried.

"It's coming from up there somewhere!" George whispered loudly. He scanned the night sky.

I frowned. "There's something weird about that dragon's roar," I said slowly.

"What do you mean?" Ashley whispered.

"It's exactly the same sound, over and over," I said. "Almost like—a recording. Listen!"

"AAUUGGHH! AAAUUUGGHH!"

"You're right, Mary-Kate!" Uncle Josh declared.

Ashley gasped. “I know. It’s coming from the loudspeakers!” she cried, pointing at one of the poles that held the speakers.

“Then whoever is doing it must be in my office!” Uncle Josh declared. “Come on!”

We all raced across the dusty yard and into the lodge. We piled into Uncle Josh’s office. “All right, cut it out, whoever you are!” Uncle Josh yelled. “We’ve caught you red-handed!”

But there was no one there! The office was empty and silent. Screen-saver fish swam slowly across Uncle Josh’s computer screen.

I checked behind the door. Ashley looked under the desk. George yanked open the door of the supply closet.

No one.

“That’s funny,” Uncle Josh said. “I’m almost positive I turned off my computer before I left the office tonight. But now it’s back on.”

"Really?" Ashley said. She crossed to the computer and pressed a key.

The screen saver vanished. I could see a message on the screen: REMOTE ACCESS SUCCESSFUL.

"What does that message mean?" I asked, confused.

"It means someone logged on to my computer from somewhere else!" Uncle Josh said, frowning. "Whoever was making those sounds did it from their own computer and sent it to my computer electronically!"

Another message flashed across the screen: LOGGING OFF, GOOD-BYE.

"Now they're gone," Uncle Josh said. He shook his head. "I can't believe it. Who would play a silly trick like this? And why?"

Ashley and I looked at each other. We were pretty sure we knew *why*. At least, we knew part of it. Someone was trying to shut down the Logical I Ranch.

The question was, who?

Uncle Josh clapped his hands together. "Well, girls," he said to us, "whoever did this, it's over now. And you shouldn't be out of bed in the middle of the night. You need your sleep!"

"But—" I began.

Uncle Josh waved his hands. "Not now, girls," he said with a tired smile. He herded us out of the office. "Back to your bunkhouse, please."

Ashley and I gave each other another look. Ashley shrugged. We headed back toward our bunkhouse.

"I guess we'll just have to solve the mystery," Ashley said. "Then Uncle Josh will have to listen to us."

"Right," I agreed.

We went into our bunkhouse and sat on Ashley's bunk. Patty was still snoring away in the other bunk.

Ashley took out her notebook. I switched on my flashlight so she could write. "Okay. What do we know?" she asked.

"Well," I began, "whoever is trying to shut down the ranch knows how to use a computer pretty well." I frowned. "Ashley, I think we have to take Dusty off the suspect list. I don't think he even has electricity in his cabin. I'm sure he doesn't know how to use a computer."

"We'll have to find out for sure," Ashley said. "But I bet you're right. I'll put him at the bottom of the list." She scribbled away in her notebook.

"What about Mr. Cunningham?" she said after a moment.

"We need to find out more about him," I said. "I bet he has an office in town. Let's go into town tomorrow and see what we can find out. Maybe he's a computer whiz."

Ashley bit the end of her pencil. "I know someone who's definitely a computer whiz," she said after a second. "Andrew."

"But I thought we decided he isn't a suspect," I said. "Because all the weird stuff started happening before he came to the Logical I."

"Yeah," Ashley said, frowning. "It doesn't make sense. But still..." Her voice trailed off in a big yawn.

I yawned, too. "Well," I said, "whether he's a suspect or not, we can't do anything right now. Let's talk to him in the morning. Okay, Ashley?"

There was no answer.

"Ashley?" I repeated.

All I heard was a snore. And it wasn't coming from Patty's bunk this time!

The next morning we slept late. Patty was already gone by the time we woke up. We got dressed and stepped out of the bunkhouse.

"Hey, look—there's Andrew!" I said. He was hurrying out of the horse barn.

"Andrew!" Ashley called. "Wait up!"

Andrew glanced around. I was sure he spotted us. But he didn't wait. Instead he ducked back into the barn.

"That's very suspicious behavior!" I said, frowning. "I—"

But I never finished my sentence. Suddenly I heard a low rumbling noise. It grew louder...and louder...and then it was so loud, the ground started to shake under my feet.

"Whoa-oooaa!" Ashley yelled. She clapped her hands over her ears. "What's going on?"

7

A Not-So-Good Vibration

BAARRRRRRROOOOOOM! The ground trembled under my feet. It felt as if I were standing on top of the busiest subway stop in New York City.

CRASH! CLINK! I heard glass breaking behind me. I spun around. Two of our bunkhouse windows had shattered.

"Ashley!" I shouted. "What's happening?"

"I d-d-don't know!" Ashley yelled. Her voice shook because the ground was shaking so hard.

Then the noise grew softer. The ground shook less. Finally, it stopped.

Ashley and I stood there, in shock. A crowd of people had poured out of the lodge. They were all staring at us.

"Are you girls all right?" a woman called to us.

"I—I think so," I answered.

Uncle Josh hurried over to us. "Are you sure you're okay?" he asked. He looked really worried.

"We're fine," Ashley said. "But what happened?"

"That's what I'd like to know!" a man in a white cowboy hat called.

"Uh—it must have been a fighter plane," Uncle Josh said. "There's an air force base nearby. Sometimes their super-fast planes fly a little too low. I've complained to them about it before. It scares the horses!"

"And the guests!" somebody shouted. "Hey, maybe that old ranch hand was right

about the dragon after all."

A chill ran down my back. I was thinking the same thing.

Uncle Josh laughed—but he still looked very worried. He started talking to George and Slim about fixing the broken windows.

"I can't believe an airplane did that," I said.

Ashley was staring up at the sky. "Me, neither," she said. "Especially since there's not a plane in sight."

"So what did break the windows?" I asked.

"I don't know," she said. "But...Mary-Kate, do you think Uncle Josh is right? Maybe the stuff that's happening here at the ranch *is* just bad luck. It sure is hard to believe any of our suspects could have made the ground shake like that. I mean, it was almost like an earthquake!"

Or a dragon, I thought. But I didn't say it aloud. I knew Ashley would just shake her head and roll her eyes at me.

"I see what you mean," I said. "But that doesn't mean we don't have a case. Somebody definitely made those dragon noises last night. And somebody could have put something stinky in the well, too. Just because one thing happened that we can't explain doesn't mean we're wrong about everything."

"I guess," Ashley said. "Well, let's go talk to Andrew about the dragon noises."

But as we headed toward the barn, we ran into Patty. "Breakfast was chocolate-chip waffles," she told us. "But they're all gone now. The only thing left is cold cereal. Too bad you missed the waffles. It was the best breakfast so far!"

I sighed. Patty sure has a way of being annoying!

"Have you seen Andrew?" Patty went on. "I told him to meet me for breakfast, but he didn't." She frowned. "I've got the whole day planned. We're supposed to go riding now, and then he's going to show me how to play Ninja Warriors, and then after lunch we're going swimming."

"We saw him a couple of minutes ago, going into the horse barn," Ashley said.

"Thanks," Patty said. She hurried toward the barn.

"I think we should wait to talk to Andrew," Ashley said. "I'd rather do it when Patty isn't around."

"They sure are spending a lot of time together," I said. "I guess Andrew likes Patty—even though he didn't act like he did at the dance last night."

"I guess so," Ashley said. "Come on, let's go eat breakfast." We headed toward the lodge.

And then we heard a scream. It came from the barn.

Ashley and I looked at each other.

Patty!

8

SLIME CITY

We ran to the barn as fast as we could.

"Patty! What is it?" I shouted as we dashed inside.

"Are you all right?" Ashley cried.

We stopped as we caught sight of Patty. She and Andrew were standing outside one of the stalls. Patty held one foot in the air. She didn't look scared at all. But she did look disgusted!

"Look!" she exclaimed, wrinkling her nose. She pointed at the ground.

Ashley and I looked. We saw a dark shape where the straw was stained. A greasy puddle of thick, black slime was oozing over the ground. And it was gurgling.

"It's dragon slime!" Andrew exclaimed. "That old man was right. I'm going to tell my mom and dad!" He rushed out before we could say anything.

"Do—do you really think it's dragon slime?" Patty asked us.

Ashley shook her head. "No way! There has to be a logical explanation."

I bent down to the puddle. I reached out to touch it.

"Ew, gross!" Patty shrieked. "Don't touch it! You don't know what it is!"

I rubbed it between my fingers. "It feels oily. And there's something about this smell...I've smelled it before."

"Well, it's ruined my new boots!" Patty exclaimed. She stomped off toward our bunkhouse to clean up.

As soon as she was gone I turned to Ashley. "Dragon slime—hah!" I said. "Andrew was in here this morning. He could have put this black goop here himself! Ashley, he's got to be the one who's trying to harm the ranch!"

"I agree he looks very suspicious. But it still doesn't make sense!" Ashley said. "First of all, what about the stuff that happened before Andrew got here? Second—this is just a slimy puddle. It's not so terrible. If Andrew really is trying to shut down the Logical I, how would this help?"

"Hey, you kids shouldn't be in here!" a voice called out.

It was Dusty. We jumped to our feet.

"What are *you* doing in here?" Ashley asked.

"Dragon hunting!" Dusty said. I noticed the map in his back pocket. "I hear there's dragon slime in here."

Ashley pointed at the ground. "We found

this, but I don't think it's dragon slime."

Dusty's eyes popped open when he spied the black slime. "Come on, everybody out!" he exclaimed. He hustled us to the door. "I'll clean up this mess." He shooed us out and closed the barn door.

Ashley and I hung around outside. A few minutes later Dusty came out. He was carrying a bunch of greasy black rags. He must have used them to soak up the puddle of slime.

"You kids stay out of that barn for a while," he told us. "That dragon could show up anytime!" Then he looked at his hands and arms. They were covered with black slime.

"I've got to take a shower," I heard him mutter as he walked away.

Dusty taking a shower? "That's great!" I cried.

Ashley looked at me. "I agree he'll be more pleasant to be around after he bathes," she said. "But it's not that exciting."

I shook my head. "No, no! This is our chance to look at his map. I have a plan," I told her. I looked around. "But I need something that would be good to chew on...."

Ashley looked puzzled. "Bubble gum?"

"No, no, no," I said. "Not like that." I spotted a leather bridle hanging on a fence post. I grabbed it and grinned. "Perfect!"

"Huh?" Ashley said. I could tell she didn't have a clue.

"I'll explain when we get to Dusty's," I said. "Follow that cowboy!"

The New Adventures of Mary-Kate & Ashley™

DETECTIVE TRICK

MAP CODE

Get a map of the United States. Make sure you and your friend have a copy. Then, on a separate piece of paper, give each state a different number from 1 to 50 (New York=1, Minnesota=2, etc.). This piece of paper is the map key. Use it to figure out your secret messages.

When you're ready to send a message, write each word of the message in a different state on the map. Here's the catch: The first word of your sentence will go in the state you labeled #1 on your map key. The second word in your sentence will go in the state you labeled #2, and so on, and so on. When your friend reads the message, she will use the map key to figure out which order the words go in.

From
The Case Of The **LOGICAL "I" RANCH**

© & TM 2000 Dualstar Entertainment Group, Inc.

The New Adventures of Mary-Kate & Ashley™

DETECTIVE TRICK

WHICH WAY DO WE GO?

Sometimes detecting is like looking for a treasure. A map can lead you to more clues. And what better way to follow a map then with a compass! Here's a quick and easy way to make your own compass at home:

1. Take a magnet and rub it along a needle 30 times (always rub in the same direction).
2. Cut a small piece of cork and push the magnetized needle through it.
3. Fill a plastic cup with water.
4. Place the cork with the needle into the cup, so it is floating in the center.
5. If you place the cup on a flat surface, the needle will always point north.

Try it!

Look for our next mystery...
The Case Of The **DOG CAMP MYSTERY**

9

SUSPECT ROUND-UP

We tailed Dusty back to his cabin. We hid behind his pickup truck while he went inside. Finally we heard two things that let us know he was in the shower: number one, the sound of splashing water, and number two, the sound of really bad singing.

"'Oh, my darlin', Oh, my darlin', oh, my darlin' Clementine....'"

"Let's go," I said.

As soon as Ashley and I got to the front

door, Dusty's dog came up and growled meanly at us.

"Nice teeth, Mr. Doggie," I said. Before he had a chance to get any angrier, I showed him the bridle. He kept an eye on me while he gave it a sniff. Then he took it in his mouth. I played tug-of-war with him for a minute like I do back home with our dog Clue. That made him want it even more.

At last I let go. The dog went off to a corner of the room where he could be alone to chew.

"Nice work," Ashley said. She'd figured out the rest of my plan already. "Dusty's clothes are hanging on that chair."

There was the dusty old shirt he always had on. There were the dirty old jeans he always wore.

And there, in the pocket, was the old map! A rag stained with black slime lay on the chair next to it.

Ashley picked up the rag. I unrolled the

yellowed sheet of paper and looked at it closely. It was a map of the ranch. The writing was faded, but I could make out the words LOGICAL I.

I found little black squares that stood for the lodge, the bunkhouses, and the barn. I saw a little circle that had to be the well. Someone had drawn a red X on it. There were more red X's all over the map, along dotted lines.

"I don't get it," I said. "Dusty said this proves there's a dragon. But there's nothing about dragons at all on this map."

"Maybe there is," Ashley said. She pointed at a red circle drawn on a spot near the ranch. "I think this is where we found that giant footprint." She bit her lip, staring at the map. "There's an awful lot of roads and trails here for a ranch out in the middle of nowhere," she said. "Unless these dotted lines aren't roads and trails at all."

Just then we heard the water turn off.

Ashley and I froze. "That's the shortest shower in history!" I whispered.

"Move!" she whispered back. We dashed out of the cabin and ran back to the ranch. We finally stopped to catch our breath near the lodge.

"That was close!" Ashley gasped.

"Uh-oh," I said. "I've still got Dusty's map! I forgot to put it back!"

"That's okay. We need that map," Ashley said. Her eyes narrowed. "I think it's time to get some answers!"

"Great!" I cheered. "But…how?"

"We're going into town," Ashley said. "We need to find out more about Mr. Cunningham, remember? And I also want to find a library. Maybe the librarian can help us figure out some of these weird markings."

The Logical I Ranch had a small shuttle van that took guests into the town of Dead Gulch. When we got into town, we started looking for Mr. Cunningham's office. A lady on the street pointed it out to us.

On the bus ride, Ashley had planned out what we were going to say. I pushed through the door into the office. Ashley was right behind me. A woman with red hair sat at the front desk, typing. On an old-fashioned typewriter, not a computer!

"Wow!" I blurted out. "I didn't know people used those things any more." I felt my cheeks turn warm. "That is—I didn't mean to be rude."

The woman laughed. "That's okay. I guess it does seem kind of strange. But Mr. Cunningham is funny about computers. He doesn't like them. We don't have any in the office."

I gave Ashley a little kick. That meant Mr. Cunningham couldn't have made those dragon noises last night!

"Excuse me," Ashley said. "Can we talk to Mr. Cunningham, please?"

The woman looked surprised. “Do you have an appointment?”

“Uh, no,” I said. “But—”

Just then the office door opened. Mr. Cunningham stepped out, holding a thick manila envelope. What luck! “Carol, can you run this over to the post office for me, please?” he asked.

“Sure.” The red-haired lady stood up and took the package. “Oh, Mr. Cunningham, these young ladies are here to see you.” Then she left the office.

“Well, now,” Mr. Cunningham said with a pleasant smile. “How can I help you?”

“We wanted to talk to you about the Logical I Ranch,” Ashley spoke up.

“Oh?” said Mr. Cunningham. “What about it?”

“Well,” Ashley said. “We heard you might be interested in buying the ranch.”

“We’re friends of the owner,” I added quickly. “And we might just be able to help

change his mind."

"Oh, really?" Mr. Cunningham chuckled. "Well, that's very nice of you, girls, but I'm afraid I'm no longer interested."

"Why not?" I blurted out.

"Well, if you really want to know," he said, "I found another property yesterday. It's much closer to the highway. It'll be a lot easier for tourists to get there. And it's already got an old deserted town on it. I'm going to turn it into an Old West ghost town. Doesn't that sound like fun?"

"Uh, great," I said.

I felt Ashley pull me toward the door.

"Thanks for your time, Mr. Cunningham. Bye!" she said.

I stuck my head back in the door. "Could you tell us where the library is, please?"

Mr. Cunningham pointed. "It's at the end of the block."

"Thanks!" We headed off.

"Well, now he's definitely off our list of

suspects," I said as we walked. "He found a new property yesterday, and lots of weird stuff has happened at the ranch since then. Plus, he doesn't have a computer, so he couldn't have made those dragon noises. Now I'm sure it's Andrew."

"Don't forget about Dusty," Ashley said. "He's the one who started the whole dragon story."

"I know, but he doesn't have any reason to want to shut down the ranch!" I argued. "Besides, he doesn't have a computer, either."

At last we got to the library. We showed Dusty's map to the librarian, Ms. Mullins.

"Hmmm. This looks like a geological map," she said. "But it's very faded. Let me see if I can find a fresher copy in our files." She led us to a set of small flat files that held maps of the area.

At last she pulled out a map. It had the same crisscrossing dotted lines as Dusty's map. But it didn't say LOGICAL I in faded letters at the top. It said GEOLOGICAL SITES.

"Wow! 'Logical I' is really part of the words Geological Sites," I said. "The letters on the old map are just faded!"

"So the name Logical I is kind of a mistake," Ashley said. She turned to the librarian. "What is a geological site? And why is there a map of it?"

"Well, a geological site is a place that's interesting to geologists," Ms. Mullins explained. "Geologists are scientists who study the earth. They could have made a map of this particular place because there are unusual minerals in the soil, or something like that. But I don't really know that much about it. You'd have to show this map to a geologist and ask him what's so special about the Logical I ranch."

Ashley nodded. "You don't happen to know a good geologist, do you?" she asked.

"As a matter of fact, I do!" Miss Mullins said. "His name is Dr. Tuttle. He's here for the summer working on a project for our local college. I'll call him right now and tell him you're coming by."

Miss Mullins called Dr. Tuttle and told him we were coming. Then she gave us the address. We thanked her and turned to go. But then I remembered something else I wanted to ask her.

"Hey, what about the dragon footprint?" I said. "Show her your drawing, Ashley."

So Ashley showed Ms. Mullins her sketch of the giant print. "We found this in a dry stream right near the ranch," she said. "Do you know what could have made it?"

When Ms. Mullins saw the drawing, her eyes opened wide. "Girls—how large was this footprint?"

"Big," I said. "That print next to it is a man's boot."

"Wow!" Ms. Mullins exclaimed. "My

boyfriend studies dinosaurs. Your drawing looks like an Allosaurus footprint!"

"Wait a second!" I cried. "I thought the dinosaurs all died out millions of years ago. Are you telling us there's one running around out here?" I felt a chill. Was Dusty's dragon a real live dinosaur?

Ms. Mullins laughed. "Oh, no!" she said. "This dinosaur is long gone. But he must have stepped in that streambed when it was still muddy—and when the mud dried, his footprint was preserved for all those years."

"Wow!" I exclaimed.

"Do you think your boyfriend would come out and look at the print?" Ashley asked.

"I'm sure," Miss Mullins said. "I'll call him tonight and tell him all about it. He'll be able to tell you if your fossil footprint is real. Girls, this could be big news!"

This was so exciting! But we still had

our mystery to solve. We thanked Ms. Mullins again and hurried out.

Fifteen minutes later we arrived at Dr. Tuttle's office. I unfolded the map, and we spread it out on his desk.

Dr. Tuttle shoved his wire-rimmed glasses up on his nose and studied the map. We told him all the things that had been happening at the ranch.

"There are bad smells coming from the well," Ashley began.

"Sometimes there's smoke, too," I added. "And this morning the ground rumbled like an earthquake. It broke out the window in our bunk!"

"It's happened before," Ashley said.

Dr. Tuttle nodded. "Interesting," he murmured.

"Also, we found this black slime in the barn this morning," Ashley told him. She pulled out the grimy rag that she had taken from Dusty's cabin. "I think it was coming up out of the ground."

Dr. Tuttle's eyes grew wide. He took the rag from Ashley and sniffed it.

"We think someone is making all this stuff happen because they want to shut down the Logical I," I told him. "We just can't figure out how they could do it."

But Dr. Tuttle shook his head. "You're wrong about that. No human being is causing these things to happen."

"Huh?" Ashley and I exclaimed together. My heart sank. Was Dr. Tuttle about to tell us that there really was a dragon doing all this stuff?

"No, Mother Nature is causing it all," he said. "All your clues—plus this map—tell me that the Logical I ranch is sitting smack on top of an oil well!"

10

STRIKING IT RICH

Oil?

"We're rich!" I cried. "We're rich!"

Ashley cleared her throat. "You mean, Uncle Josh and his partners are rich."

I blushed. "Yeah, that's what I meant."

Dr. Tuttle grabbed a cowboy hat off a hook on the wall. "How would you girls like to introduce me to the ranch's owners? I think we've got a lot to talk about."

"We'd love to!" I said. "He's sure going to be glad to meet you!"

Dr. Tuttle drove us back to the ranch.

"You know what this means?" I said as we rode. "We finally have a motive for Dusty. He used to work in the oil fields. He must have known there was oil under the ranch. He had a great reason for wanting it shut down! He wanted the oil for himself."

"Yeah, but he didn't *do* anything," Ashley said. "Except spread stories about a dragon. All that other stuff happened naturally."

"Except the dragon noises," I pointed out. "Somebody did those."

We pulled up in front of the lodge and headed for Uncle Josh's office.

Patty and Andrew were in the lodge, playing a board game. "No, you can't pick another card!" Patty was saying. "We're using my special rules, remember?"

Andrew threw down the dice. "I don't want to play with your dumb special rules," he said. "I don't want to play at all!" He turned—and caught sight of me and Ashley.

"Hey, what's going on?" he called to us.

"Come and see," I said. Andrew and Patty both jumped up and followed us.

In the office, we found Josh, Slim, and George talking to Dusty. "We'd appreciate it," Josh was saying, "if you'd stop telling our guests there's a dragon on the loose."

"Hi, everyone," I said. "Meet Dr. Tuttle. He's a geologist. We've been talking to him about the strange things going on around the ranch. And he thinks..."

"HACK-HACK-HACK!" Dusty suddenly started coughing. "HACK-HACK!"

"Are you all right?" Ashley asked.

I knew it was a trick. Dusty was afraid of Dr. Tuttle. Afraid of what he knew.

"Maybe I need some fresh air," Dusty said. "I think I'll just step outside."

Then I had a great idea. I knew how to get Dusty to admit he knew about the oil.

"Okay, Dusty," I said. "But first you've got to listen to Dr. Tuttle. He knows how to get rid of the smell in the well."

Dusty stopped coughing. Everybody got quiet and looked at me. No one had any idea what I was about to say.

"He thinks we should throw tumble-weeds down there and set them on fire. That would burn it out," I said with a smile.

Dr. Tuttle and Ashley looked surprised. Dusty looked like he was going to have a heart attack.

"Are you *crazy*?" Dusty said. "You can't do that! You'll blow us up sky-high!"

"Why is that, Dusty?" I said. "Is there something you're not telling us?"

"What is going on?" Uncle Josh asked.

Dusty sighed. "Okay, you got me. I can see you kids know what's up," he said. He glanced at Uncle Josh. "I was hoping you city slickers would be long gone by now."

"But why?" Slim said.

"Don't you like us?" asked George.

"Sure, I do," Dusty said. "You're real

nice, even though you don't know much about being cowboys. But I wanted you to leave so I could buy this ranch myself."

"What would you do with all this land?" Uncle Josh asked.

"It's not the land," Ashley said.

"It's what's *under* the land," I added. "Tell them, Dusty."

Dusty sighed again. He pulled a small bottle out of his pocket. It was filled with thick black goop.

"What's under this land is oil," Dusty said. "What's coming up out of the well is natural gas. You folks start a fire in there and we could have us a real bang."

Josh stared at the bottle. "Oil? As in...*oil*?"

Dr. Tuttle cleared his throat. "I'm ninety-nine percent sure your ranch is sitting on an undiscovered oil well."

Uncle Josh, George, and Slim started square dancing around the room. "We're rich!" they shouted. "We're rich!"

"Now we'll be able to keep the ranch!" George said.

"And hire more help!" Uncle Josh said.

"We can even buy more horses!" Slim said.

Dusty hung his head. Then he held his hands in the air.

"Go ahead," he said. "Arrest me."

Uncle Josh, George, and Slim whispered to each other a moment. Then Uncle Josh said, "Arrest you for what? Spreading rumors about dragons?"

Dusty's mouth fell open. "You mean you aren't mad?"

"It it weren't for you," Uncle Josh said, "we wouldn't even know we had oil on the property. Besides," he said with a grin, "we want you to stick around and work for us. You add a lot of color to the ranch. You know so much about the place—I figure you can give people tours."

"Well, don't that beat all!" Dusty said in amazement.

"Just a minute," George said suddenly. "What about the dragon noises in the middle of the night?" He gave Dusty a stern look. "Did you do that?"

"Huh?" Dusty said, looking surprised. "Dragon noises? I don't know nothing about that."

Ashley and I gave each other looks. Ashley gave me a little nod. Then we both turned to Andrew.

"I think Andrew knows something about that," I said. "Don't you, Andrew?"

Andrew's cheeks turned almost as red as his hair. "What are you talking about?" he asked.

"You made those dragon noises from your computer, didn't you?" Ashley asked. "You logged on to Uncle Josh's computer from your own and made those noises."

"You were trying to make your parents

believe in the dragon story because you wanted to leave the Logical I," I added.

Patty huffed. "That's the dumbest thing I've ever heard!" she said. "Andrew loves it here at the ranch. Don't you, Andrew?"

"No!" Andrew blurted out. "It was bad enough being here instead of at computer camp. But then *you* showed up!" He turned to Ashley and me. "I admit it. I made those noises on my computer. I was trying to get my mom and dad to take me away from Patty. She's driving me crazy!" he moaned. "She's so bossy—and she won't leave me alone!"

"Well." Patty folded her arms angrily. "I was just trying to help. But if you don't want me to show you how to have a good time, then forget it. I know when I'm not wanted." She spun around and stomped out of the office.

Andrew hung his head. "I'm really sorry I woke everyone up," he said to Uncle Josh

and his partners. "It was mean."

"It's all right," Uncle Josh said. "But you were pretty hard on Patty. I think you should apologize to her, not us."

Andrew nodded and left the office.

"And now, Dr. Tuttle," Uncle Josh said, "I think we have a lot to talk about." He smiled at Ashley and me. "Thanks to these young ladies!"

Ashley and I grinned. We went out to the front porch and sat on the swing.

I leaned back. "Mystery solved. Case closed," I said. Then I sighed. "I know it's not logical. But I'm kind of disappointed we didn't find a dragon."

"Don't worry," Ashley said. "We've still got lots of vacation left over. And on a ranch like this—there's no telling what we'll dig up!"

Hi from both of us,

Something happened to our poor dog Clue! She wasn't acting like herself at all. Ashley and I decided to bring her to Camp Barkaway—a special camp for dogs and their owners. We thought maybe some "quality time" together would be the perfect remedy.

Then Clue started acting even *more* strangely. And finally she disappeared—right out from under our noses. Did someone steal Clue? Or did she run away? That's what we had to find out!

Panting for more? Take a look at the next page for a sneak peek at *The New Adventures of Mary-Kate & Ashley: The Case Of The Dog Camp Mystery*.

See you next time!

Mary-Kate Olsen 

The New Adventures of
MARY-KATE & ASHLEY™

A sneak peek at our next mystery...

The Case Of The DOG CAMP MYSTERY

"Thanks for seeing Clue, Doctor Jack," I told the veterinarian. "She hasn't been herself lately."

Dr. Jack P. Jensen was the vet at Camp Barkaway, a special sleep-away camp for dogs. He looked concerned as we walked toward our wooden cabin.

"In what way is Clue acting different?" Dr. Jack asked.

"It all started back home, Dr. Jack," Ashley sighed. "For one thing, Clue doesn't chew her toys anymore. Instead she chews up our sneakers—and our books!"

"And she howls at the moon!" I said. "It's like living with a floppy-eared werewolf!"